To Teresa, Nina, Laura, Tracy and Vita

Tundra Books, an imprint of Penguin Random House Canada Young Readers, a Penguin Random House Company

Library and Archives Canada Cataloguing in Publication

Perry, Gina, 1976–, author
    Too much, not enough / Gina Perry.
Issued in print and electronic formats.
ISBN 978-1-101-91950-7 (hardcover).—ISBN 978-1-101-91951-4 (EPUB)
    I. Title.
PZ7.1.P47To 2018        j813'.6        C2017-901832-9
                                                      C2017-901833-7

Published simultaneously in the United States of America by Tundra Books of Northern New York, an imprint of Penguin Random House Canada Young Readers, a Penguin Random House Company

Library of Congress Control Number: 2017936018

Edited by Samantha Swenson
Designed by Five Seventeen
The artwork in this book was created with Photoshop.
The text was set in Omnes.

Printed and bound in China

www.penguinrandomhouse.ca

1 2 3 4 5    22 21 20 19 18

Penguin
Random House
TUNDRA BOOKS
tundra

# TOO MUCH!
# NOT ENOUGH!

Gina Perry

tundra

"Too much jumping," said Moe.

"Not enough time to play!" said Peanut.

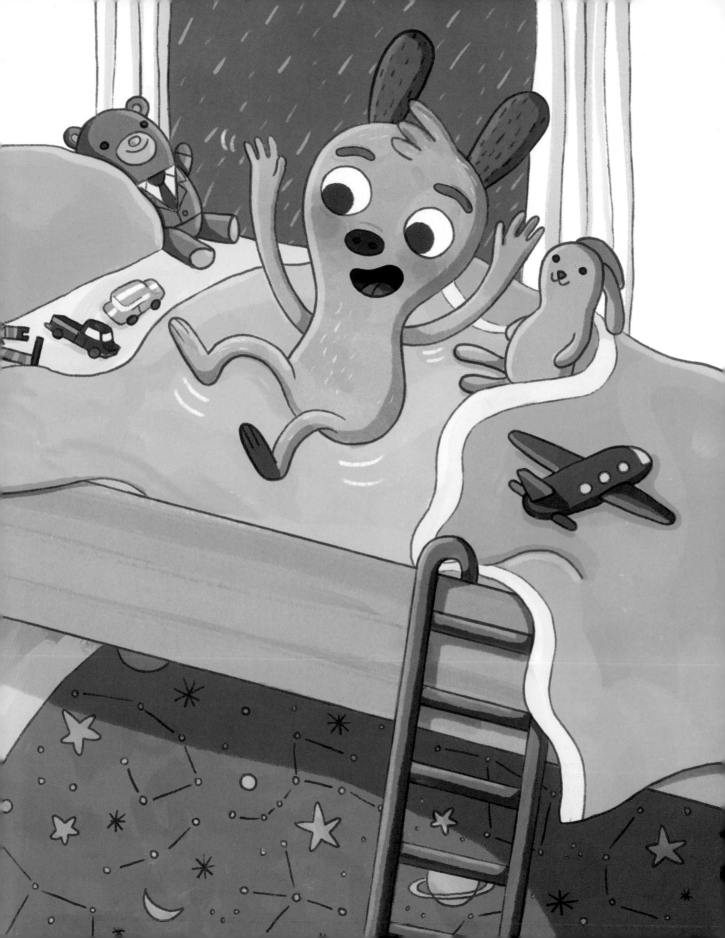

"Too much splashing," said Moe.
"Not enough puddles!" said Peanut.

"Too much grumbling," said Moe.

"Not enough breakfast!" said Peanut.

"Not enough juggling!"

"Not enough whisking
(or whistling)!"

"Not enough salt?"

"Not enough flipping!"

"Not enough muffins . . ."

"And not enough juice!" said Peanut.

"Oh! Too much food," said Moe.

"Not enough syrup!"
said Peanut.

"Too much mess," said Moe.

"Not enough bubbles!" said Peanut.

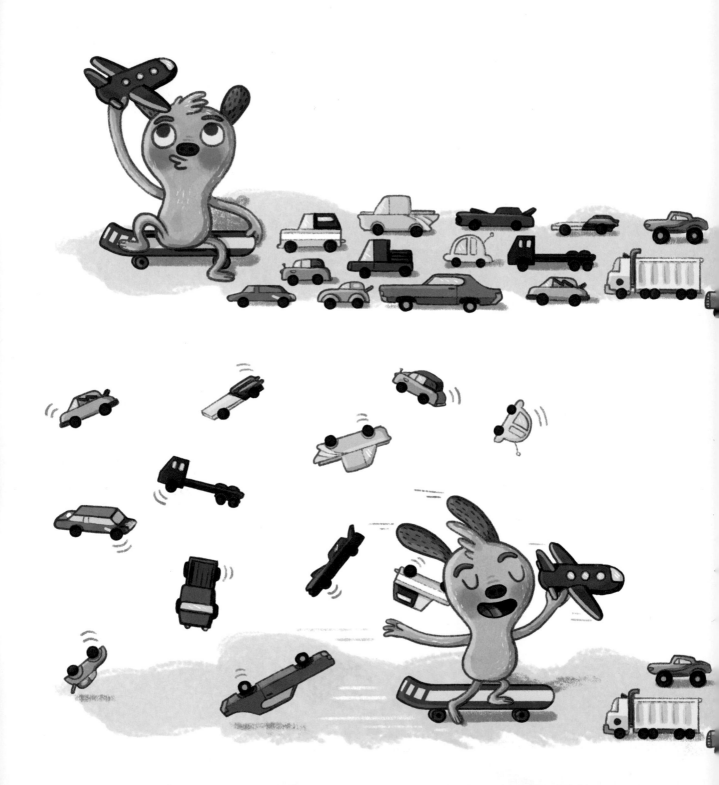

"Too many cars?" asked Moe.

"Not enough speed!" said Peanut.

"Too much paint," said Moe.

"Not enough glitter!" said Peanut.

"Too many toys," said Moe.

"Not enough music!" said Peanut.

"Too much noise," said Moe.

"Not enough kazoos!" sang Peanut.

"Rest," said Moe.

"Play!" said Peanut.

"Too tall?" asked Moe.

"Not tall enough!" said Peanut.

"Too much noise."

"Too much paint."

"Too much glitter."

"Too many cars."

"Too much mess."

"Not enough fun."

"Not enough Peanut."

"Too much?" said Peanut.

"Just enough," said Moe.